Convent Cat
Bunshu Iguchi

Story by
Barbara Willard

McGraw-Hill
New York • St. Louis • San Francisco

Library of Congress Cataloging in Publication Data

Iguchi, Bunshu,
   Convent cat.

   SUMMARY: A stray kitten finds a home in a
convent, and nearly loses it through misadventure.
   |1. Cats—Fiction. 2. Convents and nunneries
—Fiction| I. Willard, Barbara. II. Title.
PZ7.I25Co |E| 76-3413
ISBN 0-07-031703-8
ISBN 0-07-031704-6 lib. bdg.

Printed in Japan
First distribution in the United States of America by
McGraw-Hill, Inc. 1976

Miaow . . . ! This is my very own place. That's the
convent, up on the hill. The bells I can hear are in the
tower of the chapel.

Nuns all in blue live
quietly together in the
convent. They go to the
chapel very often, and
there they say their
prayers. They call one
another *Sister*. It is
Sister This, Sister That,
the whole day long . . .
Here comes one of them
now.

This nun is my favorite. She wears glasses, so I call her Sister Specs. This is the one I really love.

Oh dear. Here comes Sister Old One who hates cats.
I know very well what she thinks: No cats in convents.
Convent cats are Not Allowed . . . I shall hide behind
Sister Specs' long blue gown until Sister Old One has
gone away. There she goes!

Sister Specs is an artist. She paints wonderful pictures. She led me along the cool passages to her studio and we played. Well – that is . . . *I* played, while she painted my portrait.

Sketch

The convent garden is a most beautiful place. So much
to look at. So much to chase and tease – best of all,
butterflies. And no dogs! I skip and stamp and leap
in the air. The dew is still on the grass. My paws are
wet. Everything smells delicious.

The sisters are all in the
chapel saying their
morning prayers. They
sing so beautifully you
might think they were
angels.

Where's my dear Sister
Specs? All the sisters
seem to look alike!
There she is! The sun
makes her glasses glitter.
She has seen me, too.

I have run down the
middle of the chapel
and jumped up and
rubbed myself against
the kindest person I
know. I am purring and
purring . . . But Sister
Specs looks very fussed.
What are all the other
Sisters thinking? What
about Sister Old One
who hates cats!

Prayers are over. Sister Specs is scolding me dreadfully. She even shakes her fists. Then she looks sad – and that is much worse . . .

What did I do to upset her so much? I feel as if I may never purr again.

There's a moon this evening. The
sky is like lighted silk. The water
is clear as a looking glass. But
everything seems to be upside
down. Suppose Sister Old One
locks the convent door and I never
see Sister Specs again !
At last it is morning. The bells
are ringing as they always do. And . . .

someone . . . is . . . coming . . . down the hill! Is it . . . ?
Can it be . . . ? It is! Miaow, *miaow*, Sister Specs! I am
coming to purr to you . . .